Bismillah

THE CORD

Papatia Feauxzar

A RAMADAN LOVE SERIES

Dallas, Texas

Copyright

THE CORD

© 2025-1446 AH Papatia Feauxzar

For information contact:

DJARABI KITABS PUBLISHING

PO BOX 703733

DALLAS, TX 75370

www.djarabikitabs.com

Cover Design Concept by **Papatia Feauxzar**
ISBN-13: 978-1-947148-76-5
Category & Genre: Muslim Romance
First Print Edition: February 2025
10 9 8 7 6 5 4 3 2 1

" Be mindful of Allah and Allah will protect you. Be mindful of Allah and you will find Him in front of you. If you ask, then ask Allah [alone]; and if you seek help, then seek help from Allah [alone]. And know that if the nation were to gather together to benefit you with anything, they would not benefit you except with what Allah had already prescribed for you. And if they were to gather together to harm you with anything, they would not harm you except with what Allah had already prescribed against you. The pens have been lifted and the pages have dried."

– Hadith 19, 40 Hadith an-Nawawi

" The 'true' servants of the Most Compassionate are
...

are" those who pray, "Our Lord! Bless us with 'pious'
spouses and offspring who will be the joy of our hearts, and
make us models for the righteous."

– Quran 25:63-74

Table of Contents

Chapter 1...1

Chapter 2...3

Chapter 3...5

Chapter 4...8

Chapter 5...11

Chapter 6...13

Chapter 7...17

Chapter 8...20

Chapter 9...23

Chapter 9...26

Chapter 10...28

Chapter 11...30

Chapter 12...33

Chapter 13...36

Chapter 14...41

Chapter 15...46

Epilogue..47

Chapter 1
Azimatu

Shawwal plus 1 week

RAMADAN HAD JUST ENDED, though she was still on her period. Therefore, she hadn't been fasting for a while even though Azimatu observed everyday as if it was a day in Ramadan. She was always mindful of herself, her actions, and the people she kept around her.

Leaving her closet and fully dressed in a shiny emerald *jilbab* that went well with her radiant brown skin, Azimatu made her way to her prayer corner. Her petite form did not reveal the giddiness she felt just approaching it. Azimatu had made the small space the epitome of comfort and worship by selecting a prayer mat in lovely pink hues with matching plush pillows. She glanced at the clock on her phone and noted the time. It was almost 10:00 am. Azimatu whispered *"Bismillah"* and went unto *sujud* reciting more silent supplications and confessions to her Lord. She felt happy to regain this closure again, happy to report for duty. She felt the duty because she fully internalized that she was just created to worship Him ﷺ.

When she returned from *sujud,* she said *"Alhamdullilah"* and grabbed her French and Arabic Quran, diving right in, careful not to touch the Arabic letters since she was not in state of purity. Still, because she was a regularly reader of Quran, there was a *rukhsa* that allowed her to remain connected to the words of her Creator even when

1

she wasn't tracing the *surahs* with her fingertips. Compared to Ramadan, when she read a *juz* or more per day, her current rhythm had slowed down to enjoying just a couple pages at each prayer time. Azimatu did this to still meet with her Lord even if she did *not* have to. It was easy to come to Allah ﷻ when the *adhan* reminded us to pray, but she had realized it was harder to think of Her Friend Allah ﷻ when she had her period and wasn't praying. With maturity, Azimatu realized that friendships are built on a lot of showing up. So Azimatu had perfected her consistency for fear of falling off the wagon and losing her anchoring routine.

Chapter 2
Majid

Shawwal plus 1 week

EVERY DOOR HE HAD knocked on this morning remained unanswered. So, Majid prayed for a door to open soon because the Texas heat was taking its toll on him on this bright summer day. Wearing ankle length loose blue jeans and a long sleeve cotton canari t-shirt, he was prepared for the weather. *Alhamdullilah ala kulli haal.* The water in his gourde had even warmed. Beads of sweat had started to appear on his face and soaking into his full groomed beard a bit. The next apartment on his list was on the first floor, so he appreciated a bit of shade while waiting for the renter to respond. A young man opened.

"Hi, I'm Majid. I'm with the US census for 2030. We are doing preliminary tests."

"Hi..." the teenager said, eying him curiously before blurting out, "Are you Moslem?"

"Yes," Majid replied and quickly changed the subject. "Are your parents in?"

"No. But I doubt they would want to talk to you. Maybe lose the Moslem hat. But between me and you, I dig your outfit. Some of my school acquaintances are Moslem."

"Hmm...When will they in?" Majid asked.

"Later today," the teenager replied.

Majid had no intention of changing or getting rid of his white kufi. When he took this job, the only condition he gave was that he would not enter people's houses. He didn't trust all people to let him out alive. The social and political climate was just too tense for him to risk going into an unfamiliar homes and possibly never coming out again! *Hasbun Allah w animal wakil* was his motto. What was written for him would not miss him but was not meant for him would definitely be averted by Allah ﷻ. Majid was positive of it. He said a low "*Alhamdullilah*" for the kid's warning tip.

Chapter 3
Azimatu

AZIMATU WAS READING A page in Surah Baqarah in her decided slow-paced *khatam* after Ramadan when there was a knock at the door. She cringed. Her son was out running an errand, so she knew she had to pause her reading to go open the door. Who could it be? She wasn't expecting anybody or any delivery. Azimatu finished the verse letting out an *astaghfirullah* and then headed out to the front door before impatience took a hold of the unexpected guest.

Before opening the door, she looked through the peephole and was aghast. Intrigued, she opened the door.

"How can I help you?"

"*Assalamu aleikum,* sister," Majid said instead, smiling. She noticed his little surprised look as well as some relief settling on him.

"*Wa aleikum salam,* brother. How can I help?" she repeated, a little more impatiently this time. Her whole body played a traitor in reacting to the beautiful sight of this man. She immediately knew why he affected her so much. She hadn't fasted much lately to press down her *nafs*, and she had not read Quran as much either. Her normal spiritual defenses against these things were extremely low. Her heart had been left unguarded due to a bit of her own laziness in wanting to take her *ibadah* easy these days. Azimatu mentally kicked herself. One of her teachers always said that a true *awliyyah* of

Allah ﷻ completes a *khatam* weekly if not one *khatam every* ten days. That's about three *juzs* a day. It only took two hours max to finish a *juz* after all. He wasn't her only teacher who had alluded to that. Another of her Quran teachers said that a Hafiz of the Quran tries to read the entire Quran in six days on a continuous basis and that the seventh day is just to get back on track in case you fall off the wagon the sixth day. With her teaching job, she limited herself to a *juz* a day after work. We are supposed to live like it was Ramadan and that was feasible for her. She didn't respond to the interrupter right away. He stared at her a bit, taking her in before saying, "I'm Majid with US Census Bureau. Can I ask you a few questions?"

"I'm in the middle of something. Can you wait until my son comes back? I should be done with my recitation insha'Allah, too, by then."

"Sure."

"Do you want a cold bottle of water?"

"I would appreciate that," he eagerly accepted.

She closed the door behind her to grab a bottle of water. When she opened the door again, she was hit with another wave of feelings and emotions she couldn't canalize. Her lower self was too excited to the point of feeling sinful, and it shamed her. She lowered her gaze and handed him the bottle of water. He easily folded into a kneeled position in the *sunnah* way to drink. She tried her best not to look at him while he was removing the seal to bring the bottle to his mouth.

'*Astagfirullah*,' she repeated non-stop under her breath until she announced she needed to finish her task.

Chapter 4
Azimatu

AZIMATU RETURNED TO HER task, reading until her being was recentered. Not long after, she heard the front door open. Her son had returned from the store.

"*Assalamu aleikum,*" Mujahid extended to the house.

"*Wa aleikum salam waramatulahi wabarakatuhu* Habibi. Welcome back."

"Thanks. There is a guy sitting outside," he told Azimatu.

"Yes. I was waiting for you before I addressed him," Azimatu replied sighing with a heavy exhale.

"Why are you rolling your eyes, Mom?" her son asked with an intrigued smile, taken aback by her exasperation.

"Apparently, they started the census questionnaire for 2030 already."

"Isn't that a little too early?" he asked with a puzzled look.

"Don't ask me. I don't work there. Let's get it over with and release the man. It's hot outside."

"OK, let me put the groceries away," Mujahid said and got busy opening and closing pantry and fridge doors. Then, he washed his hands and led his mom outside. For a seventeen-year-old, he towered over his mom.

Once they were outside, it was Majid's cue to get up from the stairs he was sitting on, under the shade of the building. He approached the little family and Azimatu spoke first.

"*Assalamu aleikum* Brother Majid. This is my son Mujahid. We're ready for you."

"*Wa aleikum salam. Alhamdullilah.*" Majid answered and turned his full attention to Mujahid with a full smile.

"How are you young man?"

"I'm good *alhamdullilah*. Mom, should we bring chairs here; in front of the door?"

"No Habibi, we can go straight to the balcony from here." Without any words, she locked the front door behind her and led the way by taking about ten big steps to her right before lifting the latch granting access to her cozy and minimalistic decorated balcony. She lightly dusted her seat before sitting and said, "*Bismillah.* Please sit." Muhajid closed the small gate behind him.

"You must love green," Majid said, noticing the shades of green around him.

"I love all the colors of our Creator *alhamdullilah,*" she replied, *alhamdullilah*. Her *jilbab* was green but she also loved elegant *abayas* with rhinestones that didn't necessarily have to be green; just stylish and presentable.

"*Alhamdullilah.* In any case, I liked the view behind me when I took shade under the stairs. This is a very nice community grill you have there, surrounded by tall bougainvillea, trees, and other apartments buildings. I would have stood there for shade, but my legs were tired, so I sat."

9

"I agree with you. My balcony gives over a nice scenery, *masha'Allah alhamdullilah*."

Chapter 5
Majid

"ALHAMDULLILAH. **OK, LET'S** start. I'm Majid Robinson, and my fun fact is that I'm originally from the Caribbean. I'm also a census employee, and I'm here to complete the preliminary steps we need to accomplish so that the 2030 census runs smoothly, *insha'Allah.* I will start with basic questions." He had added his origins just to break the ice and put them at ease.

Mother and son nodded. They got the jest of it.

"What's your name Sister and your marital status?" Majid asked. A part of him was eager to know these answers.

"I'm Azimatu Dosso, and I'm divorced."

Majid nodded and jotted that down.

"What's your full name Mujahid?" he asked, again turning and giving his full attention to the young man like he was trying to make a point. Majid himself didn't know if he was trying to impress the boy or assert himself to the boy. It was a mystery he wanted to solve for himself but he put it on the back burner for now.

"My full name is Mouhammad Mujahid Dosso. I go by *Mo Mujahid,*" he specified.

"OK. Thanks for the detail. Now, are you originally from West Africa? And how long have you been living here?" he asked them both.

"Yes, we are. I came here over 23 years ago. He was born here. We plan to still be in the USA by 2030 if God wills." Azimatu replied.

After noting down everything, Majid said humming: "Interesting. My ancestors were from there; West Africa. My last name is not really Robinson; it's an adaptation of the West African name Sonko; meaning 'second born.' Since son of Robin, like Rabbi, is closer to that, my ancestors anglicized our original name to Robinson."

"That's very interesting," Mujahid pointed out.

Azimatu cocked her head, replying, "Really? *Rabbaniyyun. Masha'Allah alhamdullilah.* You learn new things every day."

"Spot on." Majid commented and continued asking more relevant questions about his task and mission.

Chapter 6
The Katib

Shawwal plus 2 weeks

AFTER MAJID INTERVIEWED AZIMATU and her son, he took her number. Every Jumu'ah, he would send her a simple message wishing her a blessed *jumu'ah mubarakah*. *Jumu'ah was* also the day that Azimatu connected with her crew on a WhatsApp thread named "The Muslimah Cougars." While Hajar lived in Dallas County, Azimatu lived in Denton County, and Afou lived in Collin County. Charles and Hajaratu moved out of his apartment in Uptown. The ironic thing about their pun-intended group name was that they had attended **Collin Community College** before it became **Collin College**. The school's mascot was a cougar. The friends had roomed with female basketball players, called The Lady Cougars. It was destiny that some twenty plus years later, they had finally become cougars in their own right. They were now older, attractive women in relationships with younger men. Or about to be.

Every *jumu'ah*, Hajar and Afou asked Azimatu if she had met someone new. They either caught up online or at their community center where a weekly Ivorian *khatirah* program was held.

The first *jumu'ah* after the census interview, Majid texted Azimatu. So, she looked forward to chatting with her sisters from the motherland and telling them about the encounter. The woman had easily formed a bond in Dallas's niche Ivorian community. They called their sisterly romance **a** "sro-mance." People who discovered the group's name found it very quirky. The sisters, however, believed it was a little brilliant.

That friday, when the first notification came in from Hajar saying, "*Assalamu aleikum Muslimah Cougars! Bon Djouman!* What's new Habibties?!" Azimatu jumped in her seat, her heart leaping with excitement. She was so ready to share her new secret.

"*Wa aleikum salam waramatullahi wabarakatuhu* habibties! Jumu'ah Mubarakah…I might have met someone…"

"What?! Spill the beans," playfully ordered Hajar. She was always the fastest texter in the group.

"*Salam*, yes! Tell us more," Afou also prodded impatiently. True and dear friends, they always matched each other's energy in the moment.

Azimatu recorded a voice message to explain.

"No, we need to see her face!" Afou insisted.

"Right, just for the record we need to see **Madame-I'm-OK-being-single**." Hajar sided with Afou and immediately initiated the video call.

"Hello? *Assalamu aleikum* sisters," Azimatu was giggling and uncontrollably lowering her gaze. She was not able to meet her friends' eyes which were amazingly both judging and sparkling with glee.

They continued teasing her. "A Mister Robinson! Look at the irony?!" Hajar noticed.

"Right? Everything was created in a pair even that name; the good connation--hopefully him since he is Rabbaniyyun. And the naughty connotation of

Mrs. Robinson, the cougar from the movie *The Graduate*." Azimatu said, going on a philosophical tangent while ironing away invisible wrinkles on her pink satin *jilbab* with her hands. Her face was illuminous as usual, no doubt because of her daily recitation of the Quran.

"The only thing created in a pair that I'm interested in for you is the one from Surah Naba. I can't wait to see you with the man of your life!" said Afoussata, being tickled and serious at the same time.

"Allah سبحانه و تعالى has still blessed you with *nur* even if your *nafs* are considering this scandalous relationship!" Hajar added. "*Masha'Allah, alhamdullilah.*"

"*Astaghfirullah!*" Azimatu interjected, "It's not scandalous yet. My thoughts are a bit unpure sometimes at the thought of him, but when I see myself enjoying visions of us almost crossing the limits, I try to shut them down immediately."

"Subhannallah! How old is he?" Afou asked.

"He is thirty-five."

"Hmm, a young horse…" Afou concluded.

"A stud indeed. But we aren't helping her by adding more fuel to her desires." Hajar said more to Afou than to Azimatu.

"Thank you! I have not been active for years and my barriers against any desires are weak at the moment. I'm currently threading a very thin and dangerous path. When I tell you my *nafs* are toying with me big time, they are. I block them in my sleep due to many years of perfecting and mastering closing the door to Shaytan, but now the imaginings just flash before my eyes while I'm wide awake. It's wild. Sometimes, I'm so overwhelmed by need that I find myself going along with the daydream before the sense to snap out of the reverie railroads me to WAKE UP!"

"May Allah سبحانه و تعالى help you control your desires for Majid, *aameen.*" Afou prayed.

"*Aameen,*" Hajar followed.

"*Aameen*! I seriously need it," Azimatu admitted.

"It's a test; indeed," Hajar agreed and recited ayah 2:155 from the Quran. "And only you will figure out how to pass...with or without Majid."

"Maybe. We will see. Insha'Allah." Azimatu said, exhaling deeply. "Well, I will invite him to the next *khatirah* if he is still around, and your husbands can sound him out insha'Allah."

"That's a wonderful idea if he can come." Afou said with palpable excitement in her words.

The friends talked more about their families, children, parents, work challenges, and their future vacations for nearly an hour before ending their chat.

Chapter 7
Azimatu

"*ASSALAMU ALEIKUM.*" AZIMATU TEXTED Majid.

"*Wa aleikum salam waramatulahi wabarakatuhu* Sister Uzma."

She smiled at the way he liked to use her nickname. She found it endearing.

"Are you busy next Friday night?"

"Actually, I have plans."

"How about the Friday that follows?"

"I believe, I'm free. Why?"

"We have a small reminder in my native community, and I would like to invite you there. That way, you can meet my people and see our ways a bit, *insha'Allah.*"

"Sure. I'll be happy to attend, *insha'Allah.*"

***

The Katib

Shawwal plus 3 weeks

Two weeks passed and Azimatu and Majid were still checking on each other weekly. Every *jumu'ah* morning they exchanged platonic niceties about the blessed day ahead. They wanted to talk to each other daily, but they knew that doing so would open a door they might not be able to close. If they aren't careful, they would welcome in *zina*. Texting once a week was the safeguard Majid had implemented and Azimatu had silently endorsed. They were old enough to know the intricacies and pitfalls of wanting more interaction. Their *taqwa* made them realize that Allah سبحانه و تعالى is watching them every moment.

"How is Mo Mujahid?"

"He's good *alhamdullilah*. He's busy applying to colleges right now."

"I see. Does he know we talk?"

"Yes, I don't hide anything from my son."

"What does he think?"

"He's happy someone is interested in his mom. Talking of moms, tell me about your family."

"My parents live locally. They are good," Majid said and added, "They are non-Muslims."

"Have you told anyone in your circle of friends or family that you are talking to a single mom?"

"Way to ask the difficult questions right away!" he replied with a laughing and sweating emoji.

"I'm 41 years old and you are 35 years old. We have to address the elephant in the room," Azimatu replied not backing down. She didn't have time to waste.

"I'm working on finding a way to tell them as this continues to have legs, insha'Allah."

"Rabbani," she wrote, using the pet name she was set on for him, "Please don't take too long."

"OK, Sister Uzma."

The mood dampened after that, and they ended their playful chatting with *salams* and *duas* to one another.

Chapter 8
Majid

Dhul-Qadah

MAJID HAD ENJOYED AZIMATU's community and had returned to it a few times when he didn't have Friday plans with his buddies. He was regularly social in his own community as well as the Pakistani Muslim Community where he took his *shahada*.

At Majid's first *khatirah* in Azimatu's community, the *imam* talked about *istiqamah*; being constant, staying the course. Majid shelved the pearls of wisdom he benefited from and waited to be introduced to more friends and family, which wasn't too long after. Azimatu approached him to meet her relatives; her aunt and uncle, who were in their late sixties.

"*Assalamu aleikum* Uncle and Auntie." He greeted them politely.

"*Wa aleikum salam waramatulahi wabarakatuhu* young man. Welcome to our community." The couple replied. They aged well in their family, he internally noticed. Azimatu's relatives looked like they were in their mid-forties, *masha'Allah alhamdullilah*.

The eleventh-month had rolled in, and Majid was still placated on the manner to approach his family about the matter of Azimatu. He had seen Azimatu's mom on a video call one day when she called her mom who was visiting Ivory Coast. Azimatu briefly introduced him since they were sitting on her lovely balcony having a quick

20

discussion about their relationship. He had stopped by after Magrib because he knew that a lot of misunderstandings happen with text messages and was worried. He was gone within an hour of arriving; her house rules. "I won't be known for a harlot around here," she explained. Since during the summer, the sun sets closer to 9 p.m., it was not too bad to receive him between 9 p.m. and 10 pm. He laughed at her choice of words.

Majid's conversion to Islam had been a point of contention in his family. And now this; his attraction to an older woman with a child. He had said no to many girls his mom Josephine had introduced him to. When she saw her plans failing, she started recruiting *hijabis*. As long as he started giving her grandchildren, she would swallow her disapproval of his new religion.

Majid did his best to call her and his father a couple times a week, mainly on Monday and Thursday nights before bedtime.

It was Thursday and Majid was dreading his regular call with his parents. He knew they would ask the hard questions, just like Azimatu did. He felt squeezed between them.

"Marcel, how are you son?" his mother asked on the other end of the receiver. She still called him by his non-Muslim name because it was hard to retrain her mind to call her son an odd name he hadn't picked for himself.

"I give thanks Mom. How are you Maman?"

"You know how I am. My eldest is still unmarried, and I have no grandchildren. I worry, and I'm worried I will never see my legacy in this life."

"Tell him again," his father chimed in the background. Marcel just closed his eyes and hung his head. He was so closed to lose it, but **he remembered** the advice given to him. When he was new to the faith, Majid regularly attended a convert care program to help him. It was especially useful to navigate the difficulties he faced with his blood relations. Listening to his mother, Majid recalled the advice **that patience is at the first try**. And that his character is what will perhaps attract his family to Islam, too. So, he did his best to not be short with them in any way, even if they irritated him on a constant basis and took jibes at him and his new faith, his beard, his outfits, his name, and the list went on.

Chapter 9
Majid
Dhul-Hijjah

MAÎTRE DIARRASSOUBA AND HIS wife
Afoussata had returned from *hajj*. The community
gathered at their residence to welcome them back
and celebrate the couple. Majid was invited since
the couple had met him at the Muslim Ivorian
Center who was just a room equipped with
beautiful rugs for now capable of containing 100
people. The *mihrab* area had been customized into
a niche with several layered beautiful rugs along
with a small bookshelf, a microphone, and some
Islamic art decorations to denote the prayer corner.
The experience was wild to him. West Africans
were vibrant people, like Caribbeans, but with a
touch of uniqueness that he fell in awe for. From
embroidered *bubu bazins* to lush *oud* smells, it was a
mind-blowing event.

Majid had been expecting a lunch served on a table
at the councilman's house. Nope! The couches of
the living room had been pushed to the corners of
the room and several rugs were laid on the tiled
floor. Men and women sat on opposite sides of the
room. The ceremony started with the name of
Allah ﷺ. Then, a small reminder was spoken,
followed by *duas* for the new *hujjaj*.

Finally, several plastic covers were placed on the
rugs to protect them from the crumbs and any oil
drops.

Following the lead of the men around him, Majid had washed his hands with soap and water, which was poured out for him from an ornate vessel right where he sat in the living room. The food was delicious. The host had served boiled yams with fried lamb meat. He loved the *daguaba*; the big round dishes of food that everyone communally ate from. Each big plate had a group of men huddled around it, eating voraciously with their hands. The delicious sauce accompanying the meat reminded him a bit of a Jamaican dish. When he was full, he licked his fingers and washed his hands like everyone else. From afar, he could tell that it was the same setting for the women. Azimatu was amongst them, and his heart flipped every time his eyes fell on her in the gathering.

At the end of the gastronomic segment, the hosts thanked their guests, and everyone leisurely dispersed. Majid waited outside to see if he could greet and talk to Uzma before leaving.

While waiting outside under the five-o'clock Texas sun, his eyesight fell on the small open shopping chic mall across the two large streets separating the gated community from the mundane life of Mckinney. Majid wasn't an obsessive shopper, so the name brands didn't faze him. What phased him was the romantic vibe of the area. It was an ideal spot for a casual stroll with a loved one. Large basins of water, fountains, colorful trees, pocket prairies and the like adorned the space, and he could easily spot them in the distance. Then an idea struck him.

"*Assalamu aleikum,* I'm outside. I want to see you before I leave. Better, I want to take a casual stroll with you across the street. We can digest the food we ate by the same token."

"Sure. I will be right out," was her speedy response.

Chapter 9
Majid

Muharram

AS THE ISLAMIC NEW Year ushered in, the community wished each other a happy new year and extended *duas* to one other for prosperity, high *eeman,* and long healthy lives. That month, it was Hajar and Tariq's turn to invite their friends over to break the fast with them in honor of Ashura. Falling on a weekday, the community agreed to commemorate the event the upcoming weekend.

Majid had been in different parts of the state because of his job. It allowed him to observe the characteristics of each city of North Texas. The part of town he had been invited to for Ashura dinner, Northpark in Uptown, was known for having many thick green trees and large castle-like dwellings. While there were also many chic and expensive townhomes in the area, his hosts lived on a quiet street with mailboxes lining it in front of each McMansion. A saying Majid had heard around the Ivorians popped into his mind while he took in his posh surrounding; *"Les moutons se promènent ensemble mais ils n'ont pas le même prix."* The lambs hang out together, but they don't have the same price. Before envy settled in his heart, he whispered; *"Masha'Allah!"* It was more to himself than anything else. He parked his car, adding it to the multitude of cars already in the driveways and along the road.

The host Tariq greeted Majid at the door.

"*Assalamu wa aleikum* Brother, please come in."

"*Wa aleikum salam,* thank you!" The other guests were already there. He joined the light conversation until *iftar* was served and then the host turned his attention to Majid.

"Did you check out that Islamic library in Richardson I recommended?" Tariq asked Majid.

"Yeah, it's vast, *subhannallah*. But I didn't find the book I was looking for there. That said, the librarian took the name of the book and will try to get it from his book dealer in Cairo, *insha'Allah*."

"Perfect," Tariq replied, passing the pounded yam plate to Charles so he could serve himself.

"Thanks," said Choualiyou and then he passed the plate to Majid. Majid couldn't help what he said next addressing his host Tariq. "So, your chef cooks all the dishes?"

"On days he is out, I cook sometimes, or we eat leftovers from his previous batches," Tariq answered. He shrugged his shoulders and served himself a heaping portion of a tasty okra stew with a ladle filled with all types of meats: crab, *pgôlô* (beef skin), fish, and beef meat.

"Interesting," Majid pinned. Azimatu cleared her throat from the other end of the table where she was sitting with the other two women. And that was his cue to shut down that discussion. They exchanged an inaudible conversation with their eyes that everyone noticed, creating a brief moment of awkwardness before they resumed the lively discussion around other mundane topics.

Chapter 10
Azimatu
Safar

Majid's mother invited Azimatu for tea and was surprised to see that she wasn't dealing with a wrinkled woman.

"Because of *halal* food restrictions, I insist on coming only for afternoon tea so that I don't subject the elder woman to a lot of cooking. Plus, I'm very picky on what I consume. There is a high chance I won't like traditional Caribbean food right off the bat." Azimatu had pointed out to Majid after being informed of the invite.

"Women..." he shook his head. "I ate your food without any complaints," he said, looking a bit hurt by her words.

"I know Rabbani. But I don't look this young because I consume *everything*," she said, sweetly, batting her eyelashes at him. The *haram* police would have hanged her if they had witnessed this moment.

"Fine!" he grumbled, letting her win.

At his petite and greying mom's place which was at a cozy family home in Richardson, after the formal introduction, Majid's mother spoke while his tall and handsome father with the Nubian nose and darker skin tone just smiled. They were equally older, like Azimatu's relatives at the Ivorian *masjid*. His parents were in their early seventies for sure, she concluded.

"Are you sure you aren't 26?" Majid's mother asked Azimatu, pleasantly surprised that her son's interest didn't look her age. Her biological clock was ticking but nobody had anything on her about her looks. Since she was non-Muslim, Majid knew he couldn't share a picture of Uzma with his mother or with other *non-mahrams* from the get-go. Azimatu smiled and all resistance dissipated here on out between his family and her.

After their successful first exchange, Majid's mother started supporting his relationship with Uzma. The only hurdle was the pressure she subjected them to; "Get married soon and get busy. I want my grandchildren!" Her comments made Azimatu, who was shy, lower her head and giggle uncontrollably like a girl. She focused her gaze on the rug facing her and whipped her head around from time around the room. They were seated in the *salon*; in the true French sense of the word. The open kitchen facing them led to the garage door. The house was a two-story house where the upstairs led to more rooms, bathrooms, and a game room. She passed them when she asked to use the restroom. The restroom downstairs was being used. And the only other one on the first floor was in the host's bedroom so she couldn't use that restroom. Azimatu finally noticed that the windows next to the salon that gave on the well-trimmed grass in the expansive backyard.

Chapter 11
The Khatib
Rabbi One

AZIMATU AND MAJID CONTINUED a low maintenance checking in on each other for six months until winter rolled in and brought along the seasons of parties. The local Arab *masjid* Azimatu attended had several appreciation events in honor of their regular donors. She was invited to many different dinners and had invited Majid to a donor appreciation event. Normally, she went alone or with her son. She was ecstatic because his presence would remove the attention of the other women from her. Lowkey or with overt aggression, most married women feared attractive and devoted single women like Azimatu in the Muslim community. Usually, she acted like she didn't notice their stares, microaggressions, or knowing looks. She simply kept her head down, ate, and talked to any cordial body at her table. This year, it would be different.

They non-couple arrived in different cars but sat at the same table.

"*Assalamu aleikum*, Sister Azimatu," he greeted her in the parking lot. His dashing smile matched his crisp thobe.

"*Wa aleikum salam waramatulahi, Brother* Majid. How are you doing on this wonderful chilly night?" she asked as he held open the door to her Mercedes Benz.

"*Alhamdullilah*, sister. Not bad. How are you dear sister?"

As they continued their niceties and small talk, more guests arrived and parked. Without dallying outside too much, because the cold air was too nippy, they quickly trudged inside. As soon as they stepped into the hall the sisters who knew her along with some nosey brothers had questioning looks on their faces.

'Are you surprised?' the look she flashed back asked. Not hiding a grin, she was satisfied that she was winning. At that same moment, Azimatu asked Allah سبحانه و تعالى to forgive her for the satisfaction she was feeling. *Ya Rabb! Help me not cross your boundaries, aameen.*

In the event room, most families and acquaintances huddled together around the same table.

"*Assalamu aleikum,* brother!" a man in the room zeroed in on them. "Did you finally steal one of the jewels of our community? We didn't hear about a marriage."

The question took Majid by surprise, but he was equally quick and sharp in his response.

"Well, she is off the market for sure. Brother...?"

"Brother Bashir! Nice to meet you Brother...?"

"Majid. My name is Majid."

Majid continued to field a lot of questions around his relationship with Azimatu. Some people even asked him straight up why he was interested in an older woman with a child. He continued to dodge them diplomatically without being concise in any responses.

Azimatu also received some landmines. What was the alternative way to deal with all the assumptions? Say that they were on a date? The community would collectively lose their minds because Azimatu and Majid knew better than to be on a date, especially at a mosque function! So, both smiled at each other's resourcefulness at dodging landmines and continued to enjoy their dinner.

Chapter 12
The Khatib

Rabi Two

AZIMATU TOLD MAJID TO get straight to the point. She asked him what he was looking for in a spouse. Majid's list was too traditional and somewhat naive for Azimatu because at this point in her life her devotion was her priority.

"Well, I want a spouse who can cook for me regularly. A wife who can clean and a wife who still rear children and manage our finances."

"Basically, you want a secretary," Azimatu cut in sharply as they were having a talk on her balcony one evening after they had a dinner, which she had managed to scramble up for them. Thankfully, the baked potatoes with colorful bell peppers along with the fried chicken with the spicy deep were easy enough to make, whip, and serve in a record's time. If there was one thing Azimatu hated besides idle time, it was long hours cooking in the kitchen. She saw long hours of cooking as a waste of time. Her budget of time principle in the kitchen is that she should never have to spend more than hour in the kitchen.

"It sounds bad when you put it that way Uzma. I know many people who don't see any issues with these tasks," Majid pointed out. His stance on a woman cooking for him was the reason they had "that eye talk" when Tariq mentioned his Chef or himself cooking for his wife Hajar. Azimatu blocked him from voicing his opinion that day to her friends. It wasn't the time for that.

"Hmm," is all she said and then added, "what time will I consecrate to my Lord if you are intent on eating my cooking all day every day? She was a dessert queen of no-baked goodies, but that didn't mean she enjoyed standing in the kitchen for long hours at length. Her son learned to cook at ten years old because he knew that his mom needed the constant watering of the Quran to love him. She needed a lot of pouring into her own cup to have the bandwidth to love him. Mo Mujahid made the correlation easily. If Mom had more time with Quran, she loved him more, but she had less time with Quran, she was on edge. Consequently, she was less affectionate towards him. So, he decided to do his part; help his Mom love him better. *Alhamdullilah.*

Back to the lovers, Majid continued to convince Azimatu to no avail for the umpteenth time until they switched to the topic of children for the umpteenth time as well. Majid was still prime to have children. And he wanted them as soon as possible. Azimatu wanted them but she had her reservations she didn't voice. Their relationship had become a landmine of touchy subjects she wished she could avoid at all costs.

While Azimatu was thin on love bandwidth with children, her two friends Hajar and Afou were busy lining up pregnancies. Hajar was in her second pregnancy after two years of marriage. Afou was also pregnant. Reflecting on their situations and knowing that she might be in their shoes on, it dawned on her that Allah سبحانه و تعالى perhaps blessed Khadijah رضي الله عنها with almost all the children of the Prophet ﷺ to show to people that older can have many children, too! The *azwaj mutahharah* were younger and logically the best bet for children bearing. But Allah decided only that Khadijah رضي الله عنها and the concubine will bear his ﷺ's children. That amazing realization awakened Azimatu and deepened her awe of Her Creator; *signs for people of thought indeed,* she inferred. Even the examples of Prophet Ibrahim and Zachariyah *aleihum salaam* were also great examples of old folks rearing children only His Might!

Snapping out of her reverie while standing in her kitchen, Azimatu reached out to the scented orchid vanilla hand soap bottle to get a dollop before bringing her hands to the faucet for a quick handwashing. She was stressed by love and babies, that she actually wanted to bake a cake to numb her racing mind with some baking math.

Chapter 13
Majid

Jumada One

MAJID SAW AZIMATU'S unwillingness to sacrifice for him as a lack of care and love for him. He was hurt. He said, "When you love someone, you don't make excuses. You simply do things for them. You learn their love language."

"You're right. I Love Allah سبحانه و تعالى more," Azimatu said, lowering her gaze. "Instead of wasting each other's time, let's do *istikhara* and take a compatibility test." She suggested.

Majid agreed and left her place somberly that night.

***

Azimatu

The next day on Friday, when she arrived home from a normal day of work, she quickly washed her hands as usual and directly turned her longing to her Lord like surah 94 verse 8 advises. She read the Quran and did some *adhkar*. When Azimatu felt a bit calm, she pulled out her diary and started logging a love letter. It was an emotionally-charged love letter she knew he would never read.

Majiiid, she wrote with the inaudible moan resonating in her own head. *Majiid.* She repeated the sensual moan in her head again. She did that again and again until she was satisfied. *Ugh! You drive me insane,* she finally whispered on the brink of ecstasy and climax. *Every bit of me is yearning for your touch, for your kisses, for your full attention. I have imagined hajj and umrah with you. It's so vivid in my mind that I deny the fact that it can't be real. I have also imagined sweet and tender love in your arms. I have imagined your warm embrace around me even if we have never hugged. The point is I can't imagine a life with another man. When I meet or see a man who can fit the profile I am looking for, I make myself lower my gaze and ask Allah سبحانه و تعالى to only make my eyes for you. Wild, right? I don't even know why I continue to make such duas when it's clearly not working out at the moment between us. That doesn't stop me from desiring you though. I am powerless Majid. Powerless. I am having a hard time turning off my lower-self.*

Majid
Jumada Two

Azimatu had once used a delivery service for a tray of mango mousse Majid had ordered. So, after releasing her deepest emotions on paper again like customary lately the day before to take the pressure off, she decided to pay him a visit in his lair. Her conscience warned her that it was seeking trouble and foolish, but she ignored the voices. *We behave ourselves in my place all along, insha'Allah it will be fine.* So, she went ready to confront him and make him understand her side of the story. It was a Saturday morning and she knew he would be home. Majid lived in a decent gated community where he rented a room in a family house with other tenants. When she arrived there, Azimatu knew she had been there. She wracked her mind to try to remember when until it hit. One of her hot dreams she had recently, had been a place like that. She had even forgotten it. Now, it came like a punch to her heart. She clearly remembered how he deliberately kissed her in her dream, and she didn't stop him. When they were they satisfied of the passionate kiss, they exchanged some words she couldn't remember and took vacancy of each other's companies! *Subhanallah, our souls met! Allahu Akbar. You should turn around before it becomes reality,* a voice in her warned. She dismissed it and proceeded to knock at his main door. A tenant she didn't know opened and she explained her business there.

"Hi there, I'm here to see Majid."

He looked at her curiously and said, "you mean Marcel?"

"Huh?"

"You look Muslim. The only Muslim tenant here is Marcel. Hold on, let me go get him," he said and closed the door gently.

"OK…"

A few minutes later, Majid emerged surprised. "What brings you here?"

"Can we speak privately?" she asked.

"Of course. Come in"

She followed him to his bedroom. She immediately noticed how half a wall divided his bed was from his personal sitting area. His wooden queen bed was made with grey and white sheets. A bedside commode took domicile one side of the bed with a chic black lamp posing on it. His cellphone, keys, and wallet kept company to the tall lamp, besides it.

On the other side of the half-wall in his room studio, there was a small sitting arrangement of three comfy chairs and an average size flat screen TV on which a match of soccer followed its course.

"Have a seat," he offered and Azimatu sat.

After Majid sat, she cleared her throat and launched into a tale.

"My parents had a beautiful marriage until my father passed away. So, I always wanted something like their love, dedication, and commitment. I thought I had found that in my very traditional ex. My ex-husband lied to me about money, about his previous marriage, about a lot of things. I was devoted to him. I cooked. I cleaned. I sacrificed my career for him until all his lies caught up to us and it was a bitter pill to swallow. So, I swore I would never serve a man like that again. And that I would prioritize my relationship with God first. I blamed myself for putting a creation before the Creator. This is why I'm the way I'm. Why aren't you married at your age?"

"Coming from the background I come, we date before committing. My parents were high school sweethearts. They didn't get married until they finished college. Once I became Muslim, I cut off all ties with her because she didn't want to follow me in my new religion or make it *halal* for me. *I am very principled*, and the choice was clear."

"Masha'Allah," she complimented. "We aren't that different."

"I agree."

"I dreamed that we kissed," she said and stared at Majid to see his reaction.

His mouth made an "o" first. Then he squinted. Next he asked, "did you like it?"

"Very much," she confessed, lowering her gaze. "I need to go," she said, getting up abruptly, eyes still on the floor. But she found him right in her face, chest heaving.

"I did, too. But it was a bit involved," he let out with a voice thick with need.

While her eyes were wide with alert, his eyes stared at her tempting lips she just wetted with her tongue before swallowing hard. She took a step hard and quick backed away while reciting "*audhu billahi mina shaytanir rajiim.*" Truly, the third person in their gathering was Shaytan. But ultimately, she knew their Lord, the Watchful, was also in attendance. So, her feet carried her as fast as possible out of the trap she willingly walked in while Majid stood there dumbfounded.

Chapter 14
The Katib
Rajab

SO, MAJID AND AZIMATU took a compatibility test. They were compatible for the most part *masha'Allah alhamdullilah* except for the spousal duties and children rearing parts. And this wasn't a surprise to either of them. This was the part they were advised to work on if they wanted their relationship to have any legs to stand on and succeed.

In the end, Azimatu and Majid tried to talk to an Imam to try to find common ground with their diverging views on spousal duties. In the end, the Imam gave them both a verdict.

"Brother Majid, Sister Azimatu is not required to serve you. It's commendable if she does but it seems she has other priorities, and you are not at the top of those priorities even if she deeply cares for you. May Allah سبحانه و تعالى help you find the perfect fit. *Aameen.* This match is right *masha'Allah,* but it's not perfect," he said, looking at the pained face Azimatu displayed.

She always said, "Love is not enough."

"Sister Azimatu, may Allah سبحانه و تعالى make it easy for you, too." Azimatu nodded, unable to voice any words.

The Khatib
Shaban

THE MONTH OF SHABAN THAT year was agonizing for our lovebirds. Majid and Azimatu had stopped communicating because of their differences. The first week, Azimatu really missed seeing Majid at the Monday *halaqas* of her local *masjid*. That night she went to bed heart shredded and broken. She was still hopeful of seeing him later during the week. However, he also didn't show up at the Friday's circle of her Ivorian community weekly get together. Early that Jumu'ah, she had patiently awaited his regular "blessed jumu'ah" message accompanied with *duas*. She waited in vain for the message to materialize itself. For the first time in her life, she was annoyed when the Cougars' well-wishing messages came in. She was deflecting her anger, and she knew it. Through it she upheld her normal character and behaved as she should. *Astaghfirullah*, she said to herself later. Look at how this man is making react to my friends. *Subhanallah!* It scared her.

One week went that way with no sign of life from Majid. It was suddenly harder to navigate her daily life without his presence. However, at each *salah* time, Azimatu managed to put her worldly desires asides.

She truly shed them for the numerous meetings she had with her Lord daily for she always exhaled deeply and said before any *salah,* "Ya Allah, help me forgot *dunya* and only focus on you," as she lifted her hands just above her chest ready to let the *takbir* and start her office time with Allah سبحانه و تعالى. For the promise of seeing His face one day, she numbed her feelings and prayed each prayer as it was her only shot. She tried to have *Ihsan* in her

42

worship; by worshipping Allah سبحانه و تعالى as she could see His Majestic face. But if she couldn't see Him سبحانه و تعالى, Azimatu knew He سبحانه و تعالى saw her because He is al Khabeer.

One more week went by, and Azimatu was doing her best to keep it together. Her girlfriends checked in on her.

"How are Habibty?" they had asked.

"One day at a time. I will be fine insha'Allah."

"May Allah سبحانه و تعالى grant you patience and ease," Hajar and Afou prayed for her.

"*Aameen*, thank you Cougars," Azimatu replied with a half-smile, and they all busted out laughing, lightening the mood for a moment.

The month ended with Azimatu praying to Allah سبحانه و تعالى to show her the way; to ease the cracks in her soul. Soon, she started getting used to his absence with a lot doing and accepting the consequences of the choices she had made. Since she had lived through a separation with her first marriage, the verses of the Quran that tells the believer that He knows that the situation of divorce hurts but to still stand up and pray to Him hit her quite daily during this difficult time for *salah* is supposed to be a moment of relief, peace, a connection to our Lord to fill our cup with His Divine Love and Light. It was the gift Allah ﷻ gave the Prophet Muhammad ﷺ after the year of sorrow during *isra wa-l miraj*.

The Khatib

After the initial shock of the "selfishness" of Azimatu settled in, Majid became very sad. He didn't want go to work for a couple days. Kowing himself, he didn't want to be found walking aimlessly in the streets of Dallas and being hit by a car as a result because he was out of it. So, he called in sick. Sick with love. The first person he had called was his Mom.

"Maman, can you believe it? She doesn't want to cater to a man anymore because she is busy praying the majority of the time!"

"While I want to hang her for it, the Lord comes first my son," his mother said tactfully.

"Which side are you on Mamam?!"

"Yours of course! But she has a valid point."

Majid made a disapproving clucking sound and requested to talk to his father. His father just listened to him and in the end said, "Son, it will be OK. You will make it."

Not feeling their support at all, Majid did his best to not lose his temper with them and ended the call with them.

After three days of mopping around his apartment while struggling to get his *salah* in at each appointment, anger and feelings of confrontation sparked in his heart. This was enough to fuel his muscles to return back to work. Majid stayed mad like for another week. He didn't call his parents because he felt like they betrayed him and because he wanted some space. He tried to hang out with his *masjid* crew and decent non-Muslim friends he still had to forget the sting. Fearing they would react like his parents did, he didn't bring up the issue to them. Besides, how was he going to explain the relationship without it coming up like a *haram* relationship since there is no dating in Islam. Azimatu and him weren't married. They didn't cross any intimate no-no because of their *taqwa* but nobody would understand that they could control themselves because they didn't want to disgrace themselves and take away the favors He 🕸 had bestowed upon them. They knew better than to trade Allah's closeness for a fleeting moment of flesh.

When his feeling of anger finally subsided, sadness took a hold of him again. It's then he realized that he hadn't told the Being he needed to bring the issue to all along because he was busy with his ego. So, when the realization hit him, he went straight in *sujud* and said, "Ya Allah, I have wronged myself. If you don't forgive me, I will certainly be of the wrongdoers. Ya Allah, I love your beloved servant Azimatu. However, I think she is a bit over the top with her worship. Please incline her heart to make time for me if you decide to join me in holy matrimony with her. Ya Allah please. Ya Allah I have no need or intention to compete with You. I will never win this fight. Ya Allah, I just want her as my cover and I want to be her cover. *Astaghfirullah*. Please answer my *duas*, please don't return my hands empty Ya Rabb, *aameen*."

Chapter 15
Azimatu

Ramadan

At last, Azimatu concluded that she was well off without a man. Yes, she missed a man's attention and warmth. However, the man who will not mind her long reading sessions of Quran, her daily *hifz*, and her continuous seeking of knowledge had not come to her doorstep yet. So, for now, she would do her best to remove Majid from her system. His sight enflamed her whole being so much that it scared her. *I will not follow my desires. Ya Allah, help me curb this desire,* she prayed and went in *sujud* sobbing. *Everyday is Ramadan for me…*

After that prayer, it felt like a bug bit her. Azimatu was suddenly energized by a message from Majid.

"I can cook and clean. Can you please meet half-way? Meet you at your door in an hour."

Azimatu smiled and started cleaning her apartment like a tornado in reverse. Majid never sat for too long in her living room, but she acted like he was sleeping over. She agonized over the fact that he might need to use the bathroom and it would be dirty. And that she had no snacks to offer him in case he was hungry! She had no idea how a 180 flip had occurred in her. *Allah*…her mind suggested…*Al Musawwir, the changer of Hearts.* "*Alhamdullilah,*" is all she whispered as she bounced off the walls of her apartment straightening poofs and shoving dishes into the dishwasher. It was *ajib;*

Epilogue

MAJID ASKED FOR AZIMATU's hand in marriage, and she accepted. Then, he asked her for the proper way to proceed with her family. She explained that the elder uncle of the family of her father needs to be informed. So, they both traveled to go meet her mother so he could show his respects to the mother of the bride. It was early spring, so Majid wore his trademarks ankle-length loose jeans with a pink shirt this time around, a Sebago, and a white kufi. Azimatu switched it up a bit by wearing an elegant fuchsia Ankara print dress with a purple *hijab*.

The flight was about four hours. He was a stress ball, and she kept reassuring him.

"Relax, it will go well *insha'Allah*."

When they landed, they made their way to baggage claim to recuperate their luggage. Her sister and her brother were supposed to pick them up. When they safely boarded the car, Azimatu introduced her sister Naima and her brother Mustapha to Majid. They hit off right away *alhamdullilah*. While they conversed, he admired this new state; a bit old in its architecture but majestic in its own right. He enjoyed the greenery though which wildly contrasted with Texas. Besides, the license plates of all the drivers read: The Garden State.

It will be jannah--paradise insha'Allah after this meeting is over. He told quietly to himself.

Forty minutes later, they pulled up at the residence of the mother of the bride. Majid dropped his carry-on. He was still very nervous to meet someone who was stronger in character than Azimatu. He could barely handle Azimatu...he tsked laughingly at himself. *Ya Allah, please make it easy.* He silently prayed.

***

They were shown their separate rooms. They cleaned up a bit, prayed and ate. Then, they called for a meeting with the head of household and the mother of the siblings; Lady Fatima.

"It's nice to officially meet you, Mom."

"Likewise, my son. I have heard a lot of good things about you. And I have seen a lot of good signs, too *masha'Allah alhamdullilah*. Welcome to the family. I will call her uncles from her father's side and give you a number you and your family will need to contact." Azimatu's mom said as they were sitting in her living room in Newark, New Jersey.

"No problem Mom," Majid agreed ecstatic. He had the blessings of the mother of Azimatu and *insha'Allah* they will be on a good start.

When all the logistics were set up, Azimatu and Majid traveled to Ivory Coast to perform the actual ceremony. It was cheaper to perform it overseas. Their friends who were younger professionals were also able to attend. They just had to cover their ticket prices and lodging, pictures, and food would be covered. Azimatu and Majid pitched in so that his parents and some of his important relatives in the islands could travel to attend the wedding in the county of the bride. Then, the next plan was to have the honeymoon in his country, The Dominican Republic, in the Caribbean islands.

**

The Mandingue Wedding

The Katib

Azimatu, Majid, and their American guests departed from the United States on Sunday night from New York Laguardia Airport and arrived in Ivory Coast on Monday; the next day around 11 a.m. Azimatu's cousin Ben picked them up from Abidjan International Airport Félix Houphouët Boigny in a white van. Ben then made stops at seven uncles and aunties places; Uncle Mohammed and his wife housed a groomsmen and bridesmaid. Then, Auntie Anta received another set of groomsmen and bridesmaids. So did Auntie Muna and her husband, Uncle Amr and his wife, Uncle Souley, Uncle Ousmane and his wife, and finally Uncle Hakim and his wife. Majid and Mo Mujahid were dropped by Ben at Auntie Aicha's House. Auntie Aicha was the direct paternal aunt of Azimatu. When Majid's parents arrived later that day, they were lodged with Azimatu's side of the family that was non-Muslim. They would be mainly attending the *walimah* at the hotel and watching the religious ceremony via Zoom along with other relatives who couldn't attend the *nikkah* in person.

Azimatu herself stayed in her mother's house with her mom and many of her close relatives.

Azimatu's friends Hajaratu and Afoussatou were not among the bridesmaids, they were the *débah*— the sponsors of the weddings. They had their special outfits and categories compared to the bridesmaids and groomsmen. Since they also had family and relatives in Ivory Coast, they stayed with their relatives.

Majid's friends and their pairs included Ahmed and Nuha, Sanaa and Azimatu's son, Koubra and Marwan, Yusef and Sheefa, Amina and Ubaydillah, Mustapha and Rokya, and finally Philipe and Maria.

They rested well all of Tuesday and called a meeting in order at the main family home in Williamsville; the family headquarters to finalize the last details of the wedding with the family and the local wedding planner they hired.

By the same token, they got to greet the majority of the family. Then, the next day, the festivities began with the *mise en chambre* of the bride at her mother's house. That Wednesday night, Azimatu's feet and hands were decorated with *henna* by the qualified women of her community. On Thursday, the *henna* paste was removed, and she was instructed to make *ghusl* and wear a specific type of cloth print intended just for the bride along with a white *hijab*. The fabric is shiny and indigo based, a specialty clothing originally from her tribe's people. This outfit is given away to the main person who takes care of the bride in her room. An older woman by the name of Samira was catering to Azimatu. So, she would be receiving the beautiful outfit as a token of appreciation before the mosque's ceremony.

Then, the bride is brought into the living room where guests and well-wishers come to greet her, congratulate her, laud her character, eat, sing melodious traditional acapellas, dance, and provide a good ambiance in all.

When this step is over, the bride returns to her room again. In early traditions, she remained there for three days and wasn't allowed to speak; until Saturday or Sunday when the traditional ceremony took place. In recent years and more adhering to Islam circles, the bride, the groom, and everybody else got ready to go to the *masjid* to perform and witness the *nikkah* ceremony on Thursday after *zhur salah*.

For the *nikkah*, Azimatu wore a beautiful white dress made of cotton *bazin* fabric with a white *hijab*. Majid also wore the same white fabric. The mosque was packed with guests from all over the city and from far and between who either knew Azimatu's mom, Azimatu or anybody related to the bride or groom. African weddings usually didn't have a set guest list. People attended on their own volution and right. And you couldn't turn down anybody because they didn't rsvp. *Alhamdullilah ala kulli haal.*

The uniform agreed upon for the event was a purple UNIWAX print, and the colors of the wedding were purple and beige. Family members were free to buy the print and tailor it anyway they saw fit; as long as the whole family was on the same wavelength at the wedding events.

So, the groomsmen wore purple suits, beige undershirts, black ties, pants, and shoes.

The bridesmaids wore purple abayas with shiny rhinestones with a beige *hijab*.

Hajar and Afoussata wore very beautiful embroidered purple *bazins* with *hijabs* that had layers of purple and beige.

After the ceremony started, the imam gave guidance and tips to both the groom and the bride because culturally, only the woman is advised and cautioned to obey her husband while the man is left to his own devices resulting in a lot of marital disagreements in the community in the long run. Newer imams were proactive in cautioning both men and women of their duties. He also cautioned the witnesses to also do their part because they will be asked one day. When his sermon was over, he asked the questions all the guests were mainly there to witness.

"Do you accept to take Azimatu as a wife?" the imam asked Majid in French.

"I accept!" Majid replied, loudly. And the crowd roared with approval. Then, the imam addressed the wife to be.

"Sister Azimatu Awa, do you accept to take Brother Majid.P as a husband?"

"I accept!" she enthusiastically replied, and more applauses, whistles, and roars erupted from the attendees. The imam gave them the marriage licenses to sign. Their witnesses signed too, and the imam concluded the ceremony with heartfelt *duas* and well wishes *duas* for the new couple.

Majid.P and Azimatu Awa looked at each other at last with big smiles radiating on their faces. They could now do that without feeling guilty or feeling like they were transgressing. *Alhamdullilah.*

From that point on, the loud festivities were on full blast with the *djélis*—female griots entertaining the guests at the *masjid* and on the way to the hotel where the *walimah* will take place while pictures were being taken throughout.

***

Nuptial Night

Azimatu

After cutting the cake, eating, and enjoying the atmosphere with her groom Majid at their table, Azimatu was accompanied by her sisters, relatives, friends and cousins to the couple's room at the hotel away from prying ears and nosy minds. After uncontrollable giggles and words of congratulations, her crew left her. The sponsors and bridesmaids informed the groomsmen to walk Majid to the designated room.

She had groomed herself for months for this encounter she had been waiting for, for years *subhanAllah.* She had treated her afro hair and had her teeth cleaned. Azimatu even made herself a full body curry and coffee mask to remove dark spots on her elbows, between her legs and knees. Azimatu really looked forward to blowing her groom's mind on their first night and many nights after.

Majid

"This is your night man!" said his best friend and best man Ahmed in their main hotel gathering room. "Say 'Ya Mutakabir' before anything. *Insha'Allah* you will be successful and have a great child from this night."

The rest of the six groomsmen burst out laughing. One even added, "Our marabout is back!"

"Shut up! My Sheikh gave me this tip to say before intimacy," Ahmed teased back, sure and proud of himself.

"We don't doubt you." The men replied.

"Enough everyone. Thank you for the tips. It's much appreciated. Take me to my bride so I can see if it really works," Majid prodded, laughing. So, without any further delay, they took him to his bride.

The Katib

When Majid knocked at their hotel room door, Azimatu's heart raced, and panic took a hold of her. So, she made a prayer to calm her nerves.

"Come in," she yelled out. Majid swiped his card and entered the room. He was dressed in a white *bubu bazin* with the matching *kufi* embroidered in the same intricate detail as the tunic.

"*Assalamu aleikum*," he extended to her as she sat by the edge of the bed waiting for him.

"*Wa aleikum salam* Habibi," she replied, casting her head down.

Majid quickly closed the distance between them and sat next to her. Then he leaned toward her and kissed her cheek. She turned her head and faced him; her eyes hooded with love and passion.

"Let's take our time," she whispered, her eyes focused on his lips.

Majid nodded and words were no longer necessary. They started communicating with her eyes and hands. She stood up in the dimly lit room, and he followed suit. Azimatu reached out to the hem of his tunic and lifted it over his head. He in turn delicately unpinned her *hijab*, letting her hair free from the headscarf.

"Wow!" he exclaimed to the bouncy afro curls that he freed.

"I hope you like natural sisters," she said coyly.

"I heard they are crazy picky, but I can live with that." He put his hand through her well-treated curls.

"They will become hard tomorrow but tonight they will behave *insha'Allah*," Azimatu pointed out as Majid's amazement continued.

From her hair, his hand slid down her back to unzip her white *bazin* dress. Within a few minutes, they were out of their traditional outfits and staring at each other. Majid was left in just his boxer and Azimatu was in her beige bras and pants. Then, a pull simultaneously drew them closer, and they started kissing slowly while exploring each other's bodies with hungry, discovering, and explorative soft hands. Majid groaned at her touch while she moaned in delight from his electrifying touch.

They enjoyed each other from that point on until they reached the peak of their love making; climaxing beautifully together; locked in each other arms; sweaty and satisfied. Smiling at each other, staring deeply into each other's souls.

"Round two?" they asked in unison like they did when they wanted to serve each other more delicious food.

"Of course!" was their response like they did on the table when they ate. And round two was on and the many next rounds that followed until they collapsed from fatigue in each other's arms hoping they didn't miss *fajr*.

The End.

"Ramadan, the Sultan of Months. And the month of true love for Allah ❖ and His Beloved Messenger ❖."— *Fofky*